GEORGETOWN HOYAS

BY RYAN BASEN

Printed in the United States of America,
North Mankato, Minnesota
102011
012012

THIS BOOK CONTAINS AT LEAST 10% RECYCLED MATERIALS.

Editor: Chrös McDougall
Copy Editor: Anna Comstock
Series design and cover production: Craig Hinton
Interior production: Kazuko Collins

Photo Credits: Ron Frehm/AP Images, cover, 28, 42 (bottom right); Doug Mils/AP Images, 1; Nick Wass/AP Images, 4, 44; Andy Lyons/Getty Images, 7, 43 (bottom left); David J. Phillip/AP Images, 9, 43 (bottom right); Bill Kostroun/AP Images, 11, 18, 42 (bottom left); Harris & Ewing/Library of Congress, 12, 42 (top); Georgetown University Archive/AP Images, 15; Haraz N. Ghanbari/AP Images, 17; Doug Pizac/AP Images, 21, 43 (top); AP Images, 23, 24; Robert Kozloff/AP Images, 27; Ray Stubblebine/AP Images, 31; Phil Coale/AP Images, 33; Ted Mathias/AP Images, 35; Timothy D. Easley/AP Images, 36; Julie Jacobson/AP Images, 39; Elise Amendola/AP Images, 41

Design elements: Matthew Brown/iStockphoto

Library of Congress Cataloging-in-Publication Data
Basen, Ryan.
Georgetown Hoyas / by Ryan N. Basen.
p. cm. -- (Inside college basketball)
Includes index.
ISBN 978-1-61783-282-6
1. Georgetown University--Basketball--History--Juvenile literature.. 2. Georgetown Hoyas (Basketball team--History--Juvenile literature. I. Title.
GV885.43.G455B37 2012
796.323'6309753--dc23

2011038470

TABLE OF CONTENTS

Georgetown's Patrick Ewing Jr. goes up for a slam dunk against the James Madison Dukes during a 2006–07 game.

1

ALL IN THE FAMILY

JUNIOR FORWARD PATRICK EWING JR. HUGGED HIS FATHER, PATRICK EWING SR. HIS TEAMMATES ON THE GEORGETOWN HOYAS MEN'S BASKETBALL TEAM RAN OVER TOWARD THE SIDELINE. ONE BY ONE THEY EXCHANGED HUGS AND HIGH-FIVES WITH JOHN THOMPSON JR.

More than 20 years earlier, in 1985, Thompson Jr. and Ewing Sr. were the cornerstones of a college basketball powerhouse at Georgetown. Thompson Jr. was the coach and Ewing Sr. was the star center. On this day in 2007, they were back to cheer on a new generation of Hoyas. Thompson Jr.'s son was John Thompson III. He was now Georgetown's coach. And Ewing Jr. was one of the Hoyas' star players. Both generations had reason to celebrate on this day.

The Hoyas were in New Jersey playing in the National Collegiate Athletic Association (NCAA) Tournament.

Georgetown fans packed Continental Airlines Arena on that late Sunday afternoon in March. They watched as the Hoyas shocked the top-seeded North Carolina Tar Heels 96–84.

The Hoyas were going back to the Final Four. The last time they had been there was in 1985. That year, Thompson Jr. and Ewing Sr. had led Georgetown to its third Final Four berth in four seasons. The Hoyas had won the national title in 1984. That had established the Washington DC team as one of the nation's top programs.

"The old Hoyas were a great dynasty. The new Hoyas are a greater story," wrote a *Washington Post* columnist. "These Hoyas are an extremely improbable team that's been rebuilt from ashes in just three seasons by Thompson's son."

Georgetown had been a top-notch program. Beginning in 1980, the Hoyas won six of the first 10 Big East Conference Tournament titles. They qualified for 18 of the 19 NCAA Tournaments between 1979 and 1997. And they advanced as far as the Sweet 16 eight times.

But then the Hoyas began to struggle. They missed seven of the eight NCAA Tournaments between 1998 and 2005. Although they

DID YOU KNOW?

When Georgetown advanced to the 2007 Final Four, John Thompson Jr. and John Thompson III became the first father-son coaching duo in NCAA men's basketball history to take teams to the Final Four.

John Thompson III, *left*, and John Thompson Jr., *right*, celebrate after a Hoyas victory in 2006.

advanced to the Sweet 16 in 2001, they failed to win a Big East regular-season or tournament title during that span. Thompson Jr. resigned in 1999. But things did not get better. Then his son took over in 2004.

"That's not a dead program, but it's definitely on life support," a *Washington Post* columnist wrote when Thompson III took the job. But the new coach knew what he was doing.

Thompson III guided Georgetown back to the Sweet 16 in 2006. The next year, the Hoyas won their first two games of the 2007 NCAA

JOHN THOMPSON III

John Thompson III guided the Hoyas to the Sweet 16 in both his second and third seasons as coach, including the 2007 Final Four run. Thompson III also led Georgetown to consecutive Big East regular-season crowns in 2006–07 and 2007–08. The US Basketball Writers Association named him National Coach of the Year in 2007.

The son of former Georgetown coach John Thompson Jr., Thompson III grew up in Washington DC and played for the Princeton Tigers from 1984 to 1988. He worked as an assistant at Princeton before becoming Princeton's coach from 2000 to 2004. He led the Tigers to two NCAA Tournament berths before taking over the Hoyas' program in 2004. And he quickly led an unlikely turnaround.

Tournament to qualify for a second straight Sweet 16. In the process, the second-seeded Hoyas edged the seventh-seeded Boston College Eagles in the second round. At one point in the second half, Boston College had held an eight-point lead.

The Hoyas continued to show grit in the tournament. Georgetown fell behind the sixth-seeded Vanderbilt Commodores 18–6 early in their Sweet 16 game. But the Hoyas rallied to get within eight at halftime. Then Georgetown center Roy Hibbert made four field goals early in the second half to give the Hoyas a three-point lead.

Vanderbilt came back and led by one with 14.4 seconds left, though. Georgetown then inbounded the ball to forward Jeff Green. He looked to pass inside to Ewing Jr., but he instead pulled the ball back. With the seconds counting down, he fumbled the ball. Fortunately for the Hoyas, Green regained possession, split a Commodores double-

Georgetown center Roy Hibbert goes to the basket against Boston College during the 2007 NCAA Tournament.

team, and spun toward the basket. He tossed a high-arcing shot toward the backboard. It glanced off the glass and through the hoop.

"He made a great shot," Vanderbilt coach Kevin Stallings said later.

With 2.5 seconds to play, Georgetown had regained the lead. Vanderbilt got off one last shot, but it missed. The Hoyas won 66–65.

Georgetown had to be even more resilient two days later against North Carolina. The talented, quick Tar Heels scored 50 points in the first half. They went into halftime with a six-point lead. And they led by 10 with a little more than six minutes to play.

ROY HIBBERT

Roy Hibbert was named to the All-Big East team in both 2006–07 and 2007–08. The Associated Press also named him to the All-America second team in 2007–08. A Washington-area native, the 7-foot-2 center played at Georgetown from 2004 to 2008. He averaged at least 11.6 points and six rebounds per game in each of his last three seasons. Hibbert also averaged more than two blocks per game as a junior and senior.

Then the Hoyas took over. Georgetown switched to a zone defense that slowed down the Tar Heels. Green made a free throw. Guard Jessie Sapp scored inside. And Green hit a jumper. A Hibbert dunk drew Georgetown to within three points with four minutes to play.

The Tar Heels still led by three points with less than a minute to play. Georgetown guard Jonathan Wallace then nailed a three-pointer with 31 seconds left. That tied the game for the first time since midway through the first half. Georgetown fans went wild.

North Carolina guard Wayne Ellington missed a jumper with five seconds left. Ewing Jr. grabbed the rebound and the game went into overtime. That's when Georgetown really took command. The Hoyas hit three straight field goals and knocked down six of seven free throws. Forward DaJuan Summers threw down a big dunk. The Hoyas scored the first 14 points of the extra session and cruised to the victory.

Thompson Jr. was so emotional after the game that he could not speak—even though he was analyzing the game for a radio broadcast. Fans chanted Thompson III's nickname: "J.–T.–Three! J.–T.–Three!"

Coach John Thompson III celebrates with his team after the Hoyas beat North Carolina in the 2007 NCAA Tournament.

Georgetown fell to the Ohio State Buckeyes in the Final Four. But after a decade of near misses—followed by a decade the Hoyas would mostly like to forget—Georgetown had proved that it belonged back in the pantheon of top college programs. That is an unlikely spot for a program that spent most of its early history as a mediocre unknown.

The Georgetown Hoyas have been playing basketball since the 1907 season.

2

BUILDING A PROGRAM

DR. JAMES NAISMITH CREATED BASKETBALL IN 1891 AT A YOUNG MEN'S CHRISTIAN ASSOCIATION IN MASSACHUSETTS. LESS THAN TWO DECADES LATER, GEORGETOWN UNIVERSITY FIELDED ITS FIRST MEN'S BASKETBALL TEAM. THE HOYAS PLAYED FOUR GAMES IN THAT FIRST 1906–07 SEASON. THEY WENT 2–2, DESPITE PLAYING WITHOUT A COACH.

The school hired Maurice Joyce to coach the team before its second season. Joyce compiled a 32–20 record over four seasons. Early Hoyas teams enjoyed some success. Georgetown had a winning record in 20 of its first 24 seasons. But basketball was still a growing sport. There were no postseason tournaments yet. And the sport received little attention from the media or fans.

The NCAA Tournament began in 1939. The Hoyas did not play in a postseason game until 1943, though. Coach Elmer Ripley led the Hoyas to a 22–5 record and an NCAA Tournament berth that year. The Hoyas crushed New York

ELMER RIPLEY

Elmer Ripley coached Georgetown from 1927 to 1929, 1938 to 1943, and 1946 to 1949. He led the Hoyas to the national title game in 1943. A native of New York, Ripley played professional basketball for two decades before the formation of the National Basketball Association. "Ripley was an outstanding professional player in the game's barnstorming years," according to the *New York Times*. Barnstorming is when teams travel to different parts of the country to put on exhibition games.

Ripley started his coaching career while he was still playing. Besides Georgetown, Ripley also coached at Wagner, Notre Dame, Columbia, and Yale. He earned a career coaching record of 298–228. He was inducted into the Basketball Hall of Fame in 1973.

University 55–36. Then they edged the DePaul Blue Demons 53–49 in the NCAA Tournament semifinals.

Georgetown had been a heavy underdog in the DePaul game—mostly because the Hoyas had to face DePaul's standout center, George Mikan. A crowd of approximately 14,000 fans showed up to watch in New York City's old Madison Square Garden. The Hoyas trailed by seven late in the first half. But Georgetown's Lloyd Potolicchio nailed a 50-foot shot at the halftime buzzer. That drew the Hoyas within five. The three-point line was not yet in use at the time.

Georgetown then rallied to take a four-point lead in the second half. But Hoyas big man John Mahnken fouled out with 10 minutes still to play. Ripley turned to 6-foot-3 backup Henry Hyde to guard the 6-foot-10 Mikan. Somehow Hyde managed to contain Mikan, and the Hoyas held on for victory.

The win sent Georgetown to the NCAA championship game against the

The Hoyas, shown in 1963–64, only made the NCAA Tournament once from 1939 to 1974.

Wyoming Cowboys. The two teams tied each other six times in the game. Georgetown then took a five-point lead with only six minutes to play. Wyoming had a big advantage in height, however. And the Cowboys used it to dominate the rest of the game. The Hoyas lost 46–34.

"The better team won, but the margin of victory does not tell the true tale of this spirited playoff," wrote the *New York Times*. The newspaper called Georgetown's resilience "a tribute to Elmer Ripley's [team]."

It took the Hoyas 10 years to qualify for another postseason tournament. This time, Georgetown was invited to play in the National

Invitation Tournament (NIT). The NIT is the second-tier tournament today. However, since the NCAA Tournament was smaller back then, the NIT had increased importance. Georgetown lasted only one round of the 1953 NIT. The Hoyas fell to the Louisville Cardinals.

The Hoyas fielded competitive teams for much of the next 17 seasons. But then the program struggled. Georgetown was invited to the 1970 NIT, but there the team lost to Louisiana State in the first round. The Hoyas hit rock bottom after that. Georgetown went just 12–14 in 1970–71. Then the team slipped to 3–23 in 1971–72. After six seasons in charge, coach Jack Magee was fired following the 1971–72 season.

Georgetown turned to an unlikely option to restore the program. It selected a youth counselor and high school coach who had grown up in Washington DC. His name was John Thompson Jr. And despite his lack of college coaching experience, he would do more than just improve the program.

HOME COURT

McDonough Memorial Gymnasium has been the official home of Georgetown men's basketball since 1951. Although the Hoyas play most of their games at the Verizon Center in nearby Washington DC, McDonough still sits on the campus and belongs only to Georgetown. The gym is named for the Reverend Vincent McDonough, S. J. He worked as a Georgetown director of athletics and faculty member for 23 years. The arena cost only $1.25 million to build. The Hoyas' first game there was against the Fordham Rams on December 7, 1951.

Jack the Bulldog has served as Georgetown's mascot since 1962.

"Before Thompson, the school was known for only one little thing: its academic excellence," wrote *Sports Illustrated* in 1991. With Thompson, Georgetown would become known for another thing as well: basketball.

Georgetown center Patrick Ewing Sr. swats away a shot for one of his 493 career blocked shots.

3

UTTER DOMINANCE

ABOUT TWO AND A HALF MINUTES REMAINED IN THE TITLE GAME OF THE 1984 NCAA TOURNAMENT. THE GAME WAS HELD IN THE MASSIVE KINGDOME IN SEATTLE, WASHINGTON. GEORGETOWN LED THE HOUSTON COUGARS BY SIX POINTS. THE COUGARS WORKED THE BALL INSIDE TO HAKEEM OLAJUWON. AS THE 7-FOOT STAR CENTER TURNED TO SHOOT, REGGIE WILLIAMS REACHED IN. WILLIAMS, THE HOYAS' 6-FOOT-7 FRESHMAN FORWARD, FORCED A TIE UP.

The possession arrow gave the ball to the Hoyas, who rejoiced. Houston never drew any closer. Georgetown won 84–75 to capture the first national title in school history.

The victory served as the crowning achievement in one of the greatest runs of college basketball history. Georgetown went on to advance to another Final Four the next season. That marked the third time in four years that the team reached the Final Four behind star center Patrick Ewing Sr. A *Sports Illustrated* writer wrote in 1984 that those

THE BIG EAST'S BIRTH

The Big East formed in 1979 as a basketball-only conference of northeastern schools. Georgetown, Syracuse, Connecticut, St. John's, Boston College, Seton Hall, and Providence combined to form a conference that was immediately strong in basketball. Georgetown's basketball program gave up its independent status to join the Big East. The Big East has since expanded and included 16 teams in 2010–11.

Georgetown teams were as good as any in college basketball history. But dominating college basketball was not at the top of John Thompson Jr.'s mind when he took over the Georgetown program in 1972.

"When I was hired, I had a talk with the [university] president," Thompson Jr. said. "All that [he] said about basketball was that he hoped I could take a team to the NIT every now and then."

Thompson Jr. did much better than that. The Washington DC native began recruiting local players from a city known as a basketball hotbed. After two rebuilding seasons, Thompson Jr. got the Hoyas back to the NCAA Tournament in 1975. It was their first NCAA Tournament appearance in 32 years.

The breakthrough was dramatic. Georgetown was on the road for a game against West Virginia that would decide who would go to the NCAA Tournament. The Hoyas trailed by one with time running out. Freshman guard Derrick Jackson then nailed a jumper at the buzzer. The shot won the game for the Hoyas and clinched a NCAA Tournament berth. However, Central Michigan beat Georgetown in the first round.

Georgetown's Michael Jackson guards a Dayton player during a 1984 Elite Eight game.

Thompson Jr.'s first standout team at Georgetown was in 1979–80. The Hoyas tied for the top spot in the Big East Conference. Then they won three straight games to take the first-ever Big East Tournament title. Georgetown earned a number-three seed in the NCAA Tournament.

Led by two Washington DC natives—senior guard John Duren and senior forward Craig Shelton—Georgetown won its first two games. The Hoyas then lost their third game to the Iowa Hawkeyes. But Georgetown had broken through as a basketball power.

SLEEPY FLOYD

Eric "Sleepy" Floyd was named an Associated Press All-American in 1981–82, an All-Big East player in 1980–81 and 1981-82, and the Most Valuable Player (MVP) of the 1982 Big East Tournament. The 6-foot-3 guard, a native of North Carolina, played at Georgetown from 1978 to 1982. He helped the Hoyas reach their first regional final (1980) and Final Four (1982) since 1943.

The Hoyas only got better when Ewing Sr. arrived in 1981–82. He would go on to become one of the greatest players in program history. The 7-foot center was already a top shot blocker as a freshman.

Georgetown again won the Big East Tournament in Ewing's freshman season. The team also clinched a top seed in the NCAA Tournament. And the Hoyas rolled once the tournament began. They easily won their first three games. That sent them to the Final Four for the first time since 1943.

Georgetown beat Louisville in the national semifinals. The Hoyas advanced to the final against North Carolina. It would go down as one of the most memorable championship games in college basketball history. Late in the game, North Carolina led by three. But then Ewing Sr. hit a turnaround shot and Eric "Sleepy" Floyd made a jumper in the lane to put Georgetown ahead 62–61. The Tar Heels came back, though. Guard Jimmy Black passed the ball into a corner, where a freshman guard named Michael Jordan was waiting. He caught the pass, squared up, and nailed a jumper with just 17 seconds left.

Center Patrick Ewing Sr. grabbed 1,316 rebounds during his career. That remained a team record through 2011.

The Hoyas trailed by one. Georgetown's Fred Brown had the ball at the top of the key. The sophomore guard looked for an open teammate. He thought he saw one behind him, so he turned and passed. The player behind Brown, however, was not a teammate. It was North Carolina forward James Worthy.

Worthy was out of position, but he was in the right place at the right time to steal Brown's pass. Georgetown fouled Worthy to stop the clock. But only two seconds remained. North Carolina held on to win 63–62.

Patrick Ewing Sr. and John Thompson Jr. celebrate after the Hoyas won the 1984 NCAA championship.

Brown sobbed as Thompson Jr. put his arm around his player. "I was mad, hurt," Thompson Jr. said. "We'd all worked too hard to give it away like that. But Freddy had worked as hard as anybody. And everybody had made mistakes that evening."

Georgetown struggled in 1982–83. As a number-five seed in the NCAA Tournament, the Hoyas lost in the second round. But the Hoyas won the conference regular-season and tournament titles in 1983–84. They earned another top seed in the NCAA Tournament. And again the Hoyas knocked off three opponents to return to the Final Four.

The Hoyas fell behind the Kentucky Wildcats 27–15 late in the first half of the semifinal game. After halftime, Ewing Sr. began guarding Wildcats center Sam Bowie. The entire Georgetown defense clicked after that. Georgetown forced Kentucky to miss 30 of 33 shots in the second-half, and the Hoyas won 53–40.

The championship game against Houston was billed as a matchup of two of the top centers ever to play college basketball: Ewing Sr. and Olajuwon. They played to a standstill.

Georgetown senior guard Gene Smith missed the final after being injured in the semifinals. But other Hoyas made the difference in this game. Sophomore guard David Wingate slowed Houston's hot-shooting Michael Young. And Georgetown rallied from an early 14–6 deficit to take a 40–30 halftime lead. Freshman forwards Michael Graham and Williams combined for 33 points and 12 rebounds off the bench. But Williams's tie-up of Olajuwon was the key late play.

HOYA PARANOIA

During its first decade in the Big East, Georgetown developed a reputation as an intimidating, aggressive team. Georgetown's physical, sometimes dirty play helped spur bitter rivalries with its new conference foes. Opponents feared the Hoyas—a phenomenon called "Hoya Paranoia."

Georgetown was involved in bench-clearing brawls against St. John's in 1983 and Boston College in 1984. In a 1981 Big East Tournament game, coach John Thompson Jr. and Syracuse coach Jim Boeheim had to be held back by officials when they tried to fight each other. "They just completely destroy people, and, yeah, they scare the [heck] out of you," St. John's coach Lou Carnesecca said.

The Hoyas finished the season with 34 wins. That was the most of any NCAA team since 1948. Georgetown set an all-time NCAA single-season record by holding opponents to 39.5 percent shooting from the floor. It was a truly dominant team.

"Ewing benefited from the help of such a variety of athletes that it was difficult to keep track of who was doing what on his marvelous Georgetown team," wrote *Sports Illustrated.* "Georgetown won the championship with as deep and versatile a collection of players as the NCAA Tournament has ever known."

Ewing Sr. returned for his senior year in 1984–85. Georgetown won its first 18 games and lost only twice during the regular season. Dating back to the 1983–84 season, the Hoyas won 29 straight games until a midseason loss to St. John's. In the Big East Tournament, the Hoyas again faced St. John's. But this time Georgetown won. The Hoyas won their fourth conference tournament title in six seasons.

The top-seeded Hoyas then won each of their first three NCAA Tournament games by double digits. They edged the Georgia Tech Yellow Jackets to advance to the Final Four. There, they beat fellow top seed St. John's for a third time that season. "We have a great team. That's probably an understatement," Thompson Jr. said.

PATRICK EWING SR.

Patrick Ewing Sr. won the Naismith Award as national player of the year in 1984–85. That was the same year he was named the Most Outstanding Player in the Final Four. He was also named Big East Player of the Year in 1983–84 and 1984–85. Perhaps he was best known for his defense. The conference named Ewing Sr. its Defensive Player of the Year in each of his four seasons at Georgetown, from 1981–82 to 1984–85. A native of Jamaica, the 7-foot center had gone to high school in Boston, Massachusetts.

Reggie Williams was a consensus All-American in 1987 and led the Hoyas to their ninth NCAA Tournament in a row.

The Hoyas were heavy favorites in the title game against a Big East rival—the Villanova Wildcats. Georgetown had swept two games from the Wildcats during the regular season, but each game was close. The Wildcats had learned from their losses earlier in the season. They played a nearly perfect game and won 66–64. Many consider it to be one of the great upsets in college basketball history.

The Ewing Sr. era was over. But Georgetown would reload. The late 1980s introduced two new powerful centers to carry the Hoyas into a new era of success.

Alonzo Mourning continued the Hoyas' legacy of dominating centers begun by Patrick Ewing Sr.

4

HANGING TOUGH

PATRICK EWING SR.'S COLLEGE CAREER WAS THE BEGINNING OF A LEGACY OF STANDOUT GEORGETOWN CENTERS. FROM EWING SR. TO ROY HIBBERT, THE HOYAS OFTEN HAVE HAD ONE OF THE TOP CENTERS IN COLLEGE BASKETBALL.

Ewing Sr. graduated in 1985. But Alonzo Mourning and Dikembe Mutombo kept the Hoyas near the top of the college basketball world into the 1990s. Othella Harrington then teamed with an exciting guard named Allen Iverson to help the Hoyas enjoy one last burst under coach John Thompson Jr. during the mid-1990s.

Before Mourning and Mutombo arrived, the Hoyas almost made another Final Four run. In 1986–87, senior forward Reggie Williams carried the Hoyas to a 29–5 mark. That earned them a share of the Big East regular season title. Williams also led the team to a Big East Tournament title. Georgetown earned a top seed in the NCAA Tournament and dispatched its first three opponents. The tournament had added more teams, so three wins only got a team to the Elite Eight now. However, the sixth-seeded Providence Friars upset Georgetown in that round.

REGGIE WILLIAMS

Reggie Williams was named Big East Player of the Year and Big East Tournament MVP in 1986–87. He was also an Associated Press All-American in 1986–87. A native of Baltimore, Maryland, the 6-foot-7 forward played at Georgetown from 1983 to 1987.

Georgetown made another run to the Elite Eight two years later. Mourning arrived in the fall of 1988 and teamed with guards Dwayne Bryant and Charles Smith to lead the Hoyas to another Big East regular-season title. Georgetown beat rival Syracuse in the Big East Tournament final. That gave the Hoyas their sixth conference tournament title of the 1980s. It also was enough to clinch a top seed for the NCAA Tournament.

Mourning blocked two shots in the final eight seconds of a first-round game to secure a 50–49 win over Princeton. Georgetown then knocked off Notre Dame and North Carolina State to advance to the Elite Eight. It was the team's sixth time reaching that stage during the 1980s. There, however, the Hoyas fell to the second-seeded Duke Blue Devils.

Mutombo also joined the Hoyas that season. He did not play much, but for the next two years, he and Mourning gave the Hoyas what many

Georgetown players celebrate winning the 1989 Big East Tournament.

consider to be one of the most talented frontcourts in college basketball history. The Hoyas' defense was excellent too. But a lack of outside scoring and bad decision-making by guards doomed them.

"Without a good pass into the post, a gifted offensive big man—not to mention two—is largely wasted," wrote *Sports Illustrated*. "Georgetown can do everything but score."

Georgetown set an NCAA record for field goal percentage defense with 37.1 percent in 1989–90. But the Hoyas lost five conference games

DOMINANT DOWN LOW

Alonzo Mourning and Dikembe Mutombo teamed up in 1989–90 and 1990–91 to give Georgetown a dominant defense. Mourning was named Associated Press All-American, Big East Player of the Year, and Defensive Player of the Year in 1991–92. Mutombo was named Big East Defensive Player of the Year his last two seasons with the Hoyas.

A Virginia native, the 6-foot-10 Mourning played at Georgetown from 1988 to 1992. A native of Zaire in Africa, the 7-foot-2 Mutombo played at Georgetown from 1988 to 1991. Mutombo and Mourning never led the Hoyas past the second round of the NCAA Tournament together as starters. One of them had to play out of position when they were on the floor together, which hurt the team offensively. On defense, however, "the M&M Boys" helped the Hoyas set statistical records.

during the regular season. They still earned a number-three seed in the NCAA Tournament. However, the sixth-seeded Xavier Musketeers upset them in the second round.

The Hoyas came back the next season with a 19–13 record. That earned them a number-eight seed in the NCAA Tournament. But again, the Hoyas lost in the second round. This time, the defending champion and top-seeded University of Nevada, Las Vegas Rebels beat them.

Mourning led the Hoyas to a share of the Big East title as a senior the next season. But the Hoyas lost in the second round for a third straight year. This time the third-seeded Florida State Seminoles beat the sixth-seeded Hoyas 78–68.

The Mourning-Mutombo era was over. And Georgetown had little to show for it. The program appeared to be slipping. It fell further in 1992–93 when Georgetown missed the NCAA Tournament for the first time in 15

Forward Jerome Williams celebrates the Hoyas' second-round NCAA Tournament victory in 1995.

years. And even when the Hoyas returned in 1994, they again lost in the second round.

It was up to a brash newcomer to return the program to its peak: Allen Iverson. The lightning quick, super-talented guard immediately improved the Hoyas. Teaming with junior center Harrington, junior forward Jerome Williams, and others, Iverson helped the Hoyas finish fourth in the Big East. They earned a number-six seed in the 1995 NCAA Tournament.

Georgetown faced Weber State in the second round. The game was tied in the final seconds as the Hoyas rebounded a missed Weber

A. I.

Allen Iverson was an Associated Press All-American in 1995–96, when he also was named to the All-Big East team. He was named Big East Defensive Player of the Year both of his seasons at Georgetown (1994–95 and 1995–96). The undersized, unpredictable point guard grew up in Virginia. Listed at 6 feet and nicknamed "A. I.," he was probably smaller than that, but he still led the Hoyas to consecutive Sweet 16s.

State free throw. Iverson rushed the ball up court and launched a three-pointer. The shot missed, but senior forward Don Reid tipped the ball in as the buzzer sounded. The Hoyas won 53–51. Georgetown was going back to the Sweet 16 for the first time in six years.

The Hoyas lost in the Sweet 16 to North Carolina. But the next season they went 29–8 overall. That earned them a number-two seed in the loaded Big East Tournament. The Hoyas advanced to the conference tournament final. There, they led the top-seeded Connecticut Huskies by one point in the final minute. Huskies guard Ray Allen launched an off-balance runner in the lane. The ball bounced off the front rim, off the backboard, off the rim again, and then fell through. Georgetown had a chance to retake the lead, but Iverson and Williams both missed shots in the final seconds. That gave the Huskies a 75–74 victory.

The loss might have cost Georgetown a top seed in the NCAA Tournament and a good chance to make the Final Four. The second-seeded Hoyas won their first three games to advance to the Elite Eight. There they faced Massachusetts.

Guard Allen Iverson still held Georgetown single-season records in points and steals in 2011.

The top-seeded Minutemen blew out the Hoyas 86–62. The loss to Massachusetts ended the Hoyas' dreams of returning to the Final Four—much like the regional finals losses in 1987 and 1989 had. This loss would prove more devastating, though. Unlike the other two setbacks, it signaled the beginning of the end of the Thompson Jr. era

John Thompson III took over as coach for Georgetown's downtrodden basketball team in 2004.

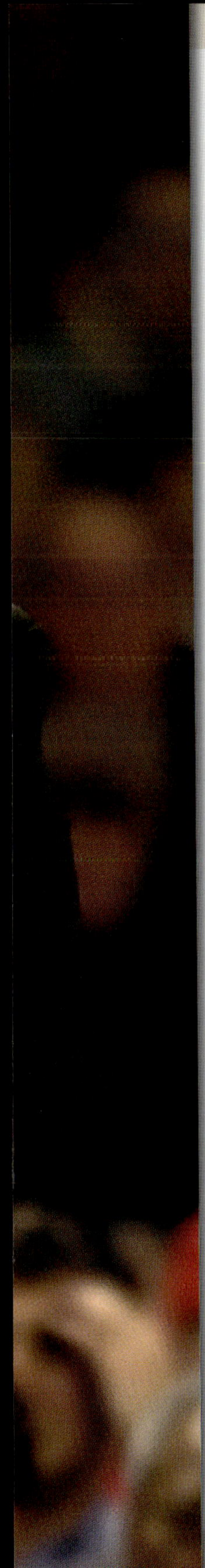

5

REBUILDING A GIANT

AS HE LOOKED OUT AT A LIBRARY FULL OF REPORTERS INSIDE GEORGETOWN UNIVERSITY'S HEALY HALL, JOHN THOMPSON III PROMISED TO RETURN THE HOYAS TO GREATNESS. HE THOUGHT BACK TO THE DAYS WHEN HE WAS GROWING UP WATCHING HIS FATHER'S GEORGETOWN TEAMS.

"There was a chant: 'We are Georgetown!'" he said. "That was something that I loved. A few people have forgotten we are Georgetown and we're going to work our tails off to remind them. It's good to be back; it's good to be home; it's good to be at Georgetown."

Thompson III was speaking at a press conference to introduce him as the Hoyas' new coach. It was April 20, 2004. A few years earlier, John Thompson Jr. had retired. And his replacement, Craig Esherick, had enjoyed little success.

The school was hoping that Thompson III could jumpstart a suddenly struggling program. Few in the 1980s and early

JOHN THOMPSON JR.

In 1984, John Thompson Jr. led the Hoyas to their only national title through 2011. In his 26-plus seasons as coach, Thompson also led Georgetown to three Final Fours, seven Big East regular-season titles, and six Big East Tournament championships. He turned Georgetown into an elite program by demanding toughness, defense, and effort.

Thompson was named National Coach of the Year by different media outlets in 1981–82, 1984–85, and 1986–87. He also was named Big East Coach of the Year three times. And he had an all-time record of 596–239 at Georgetown.

"He's a teacher, he's an educator. He tries to prepare you for life after college," said Patrick Ewing Sr., a Georgetown center from 1981 to 1985. "He allowed me the opportunity to grow, not only as a basketball player but also as a person."

1990s could have imagined that Georgetown would be consistently missing the NCAA Tournament by 2004. Yet once Allen Iverson left in 1996, the Hoyas quickly crashed. After winning 20 games and qualifying for the NCAA Tournament in 1996–97, Georgetown fell to 16–15 the next year.

Coach John Thompson Jr. resigned midway through the 1998–99 season. He had been Georgetown's coach for nearly 27 seasons, but he said his divorce was making it difficult to focus on his job.

Esherick was named coach. The Hoyas missed the NCAA Tournament for three straight years. Then they won 25 games. In the NCAA Tournament, they advanced to the Sweet 16 for the first time since 1996. But the Hoyas lost there to Maryland. Georgetown missed the NCAA Tournament in each of the next three seasons. Esherick was fired after the team went just 13–15 in 2003–04.

Georgetown center Roy Hibbert passes off a loose ball during the 2007 Big East Tournament.

Thompson III took over after that. He installed the complex, motion-heavy Princeton offense. The Hoyas seemed to pick it up quickly. They went 19–13 in 2004–05. The next season they won 23 games and returned to the NCAA Tournament for only the second time in nine years. Georgetown upset second-seeded Ohio State 70–52 in the second round. Sophomore center Roy Hibbert tallied 20 points, 14 rebounds, and three blocks in the game. Sophomore forward Jeff Green added 19 points, eight rebounds, and six assists. The Hoyas lost a close Sweet 16 game to the Florida Gators. But it was a big step for the team.

Green, Hibbert, sophomore guard Jessie Sapp, and junior guard Jonathan Wallace returned for the 2006–07 season. Freshmen forwards DaJuan Summers and Patrick Ewing Jr. joined them. The Hoyas won the Big East regular-season crown and crushed Pittsburgh in the final to win their first Big East Tournament in 18 years. They earned a number-two seed in the NCAA Tournament. That helped them return to the Final Four. However, Ohio State then beat Georgetown 67–60.

The Hoyas followed up that Final Four run with another excellent season in 2007–08. They won 28 games and a second straight Big East regular-season crown. They advanced to a second straight Big East Tournament final. And they again secured a number-two seed in the NCAA Tournament. However, the tenth-seeded Davidson Wildcats upset Georgetown in the second round.

That loss was the beginning of a frustrating four-year stretch for the Hoyas. They often enjoyed strong regular seasons only to fall short in the NCAA Tournament. In 2009–10, Georgetown won 23 games and advanced to the Big East Tournament final. But they lost 97–83 to fourteenth-seeded Ohio in the first round of the NCAA Tournament.

AUSTIN FREEMAN AND CHRIS WRIGHT

Austin Freeman and Chris Wright were Washington-area natives who came to Georgetown together in 2007. Over their four years together, the guards helped the Hoyas to three 20-win seasons and the 2008 Big East regular-season crown. Freeman was an All-Big East selection in 2010–11 and second-team All-Big East pick in 2009–10.

Point guard Chris Wright soars to the basket against Ohio during the 2010 NCAA Tournament.

The Hoyas were rolling during the next season. They were ranked as high as number nine in the nation in mid-February. Later that month, senior point guard Chris Wright broke his hand in a loss to Cincinnati. With Wright out, the Hoyas lost four straight. Then Virginia Commonwealth upset Georgetown in the first round of the NCAA Tournament.

Although Georgetown was still looking for its second NCAA title, the Hoyas had stabilized under Thompson III. He quickly guided them to two consecutive Big East crowns, two consecutive Sweet 16s, and a Final Four berth. The Hoyas had recovered from their struggles early in the decade. And they were back where they felt they belonged: among the elite in college basketball.

TIMELINE

1907

Georgetown plays its first game in program history on February 7.

1907

Maurice Joyce is hired as the team's first coach before the start of the 1907–08 season.

1939

The NCAA Tournament begins.

1943

The Hoyas advance to the NCAA Tournament championship game but lose to the Wyoming Cowboys.

1953

Georgetown returns to the postseason but loses in the first round of the NIT.

1985

The Hoyas make the Final Four for the third time in four seasons. Georgetown beats St. John's in the semifinals, but loses to Villanova 66–64 in the final.

1987

The Hoyas win the Big East Tournament and advance to the NCAA Tournament Elite Eight behind the leadership of senior All-American forward Reggie Williams. The Providence Friars beat Georgetown 88–73 in the Elite Eight.

1989

Led by senior guard Charles Smith and freshman center Alonzo Mourning, the Hoyas win their sixth Big East Tournament of the 1980s and advance to the NCAA Tournament Elite Eight. The Duke Blue Devils beat Georgetown there.

1995

Georgetown beats Weber State 53–51 in the second round of the NCAA Tournament. The victory propels the Hoyas into the Sweet 16 for the first time since 1989.

1999

Thompson Jr. resigns as coach midway through his 27th season. Assistant Craig Esherick replaces him.

After Georgetown endures a 3–23 season, John Thompson Jr. is hired as the new coach.

1972

Georgetown defeats the West Virginia Mountaineers 62–61 in the conference final to qualify for its first NCAA Tournament berth in 32 years.

1975

The Hoyas win two NCAA Tournament games to reach the Elite Eight but fall by one point to the Iowa Hawkeyes.

1980

The Hoyas win three NCAA Tournament games to advance to the Final Four. Georgetown beats Louisville in the semifinals but loses to North Carolina by one point in the final.

1982

The Hoyas win three NCAA Tournament games and return to the Final Four. After beating Kentucky in the semifinals, the Hoyas beat Houston for their only national championship.

1984

Esherick guides Georgetown to 25 wins. The Hoyas reach the Sweet 16 for the first time since 1996.

2001

John Thompson III, the son of John Thompson Jr., replaces Esherick as coach.

2004

Playing in the NCAA Tournament for the first time since 2001, Georgetown defeats the Ohio State Buckeyes 70–52 in the second round to return to the Sweet 16.

2006

The Hoyas come back from a 10-point second-half deficit to knock off North Carolina in the Elite Eight. The win returns Georgetown to the Final Four for the first time in 22 years.

2007

The Hoyas go 15–3 in Big East play to take a second straight conference regular-season title.

2008

QUICK STATS

PROGRAM INFO
Georgetown University Hoyas (1907–)

NCAA TOURNAMENT FINALS
(WINS IN BOLD)
1943, 1982, **1984**, 1985

OTHER ACHIEVEMENTS
Final Fours: 5
NCAA Tournaments: 27
Big East Tournament titles: 7

KEY PLAYERS
(POSITION(S); YEARS WITH TEAM)
John Duren (G; 1976–80)
Patrick Ewing Sr. (C; 1981–85)
Eric "Sleepy" Floyd (G; 1978–82)
Austin Freeman (G; 2007–11)
Jeff Green (F; 2004–07)
Roy Hibbert (C; 2004–08)
Allen Iverson (G; 1994–96)
Alonzo Mourning (C; 1988–92)
Dikembe Mutombo (C; 1988–91)
Charles Smith (G; 1985–89)
Reggie Williams (F; 1983–87)
David Wingate (F; 1983–86)
Chris Wright (G; 2007–11)

KEY COACHES
Elmer Ripley (1927–29, 1938–43, 1946–49): 133–82; 2–1 (NCAA Tournament)
John Thompson Jr. (1972–99): 596–239; 34–19 (NCAA Tournament)
John Thompson III (2004–): 160–73; 7–5 (NCAA Tournament)

HOME ARENAS
McDonough Arena (1952–)
MCI Center/Verizon Center (1997–)

* All statistics through 2010–11 season

QUOTES & ANECDOTES

Besides being a basketball coach, John Thompson Jr. was outspoken about social issues. He ordered the Hoyas to wear green ribbons in 1981 to raise awareness about murders in Atlanta, Georgia. He also walked off the court in 1989 to protest a new NCAA rule. And he met with a Washington DC drug dealer in 1990 to ask the dealer to avoid the Hoyas.

"I don't want dummies. I don't think they can learn my system, and they probably aren't going to stay in school long enough to be much help." —John Thompson Jr., on his recruiting philosophy

John Thompson Jr. first saw Patrick Ewing Sr. play when he was a high school sophomore in Boston, Massachusetts. Thompson watched Ewing draw a charge. Ewing later stole the ball and drove the length of the court for a dunk. "That was when I said, 'Get me him and I'll win the national championship,'" Thompson Jr. recalled. He was right.

"It was nothing dirty, just aggressive. I've been in rougher games . . . like, for instance, against Georgetown every time." —St. John's forward Chris Mullin, after a loss to one of the physical Georgetown teams of the 1980s, in the 1984 Big East Tournament

GLOSSARY

All-American
A player chosen as one of the best amateurs in the country in a particular activity.

assists
Passes that lead directly to made shots.

conference
In sports, a group of teams that plays each other each season.

overtime
A period in a basketball game that is played to determine a winner when the four quarters end in a tie.

postseason
The tournaments scheduled for after the regular season and conference tournament, including the NCAA Tournament and the NIT.

rebound
To secure the basketball after a missed shot.

recruiting
Trying to entice a player to come to a certain school.

retired
Officially ended one's career.

rival
An opponent that brings out great emotion in a team, its fans, and its players.

seed
In basketball, a ranking system used for tournaments. The best teams earn a number-one seed.

FOR MORE INFORMATION

FURTHER READING

Editors of ESPN. *ESPN College Basketball Encyclopedia: The Complete History of the Men's Game*. New York: Ballantine Books and ESPN Books, 2009.

Mourning, Alonzo with Dan Wetzel. *Resilience: Faith, Focus, Triumph*. New York: Ballantine Books, 2008.

Reagan, John. *The Georgetown Basketball Vault*. Atlanta, GA: Whitman Publishing, 2010.

WEB LINKS

To learn more about the Georgetown Hoyas, visit ABDO Publishing Company online at **www.abdopublishing.com**. Web sites about the Hoyas are featured on our Book Links page. These links are routinely monitored and updated to provide the most current information available.

PLACES TO VISIT

College Basketball Experience
1401 Grand Boulevard
Kansas City, MO 64106
816-949-7500
www.collegebasketballexperience.com

This interactive museum allows visitors to experience various aspects of college basketball. It also includes the National Collegiate Basketball Hall of Fame, which highlights the greatest players, coaches, and moments in the history of college basketball. Former Hoyas coach John Thompson Jr. is enshrined here.

McDonough Arena
Georgetown University
37th and O Streets, N.W.
Washington, DC 20057
202-687-0100
www.guhoyas.com/facilities/gu-mcdonough-arena.html

This has been the Hoyas' home arena since 1952. Georgetown has played most home games at the Verizon Center, also in Washington DC, every season since it opened in 1997.

INDEX

ABOUT THE AUTHOR

Ryan Basen is a writer and graduate student living in the Washington DC area. He grew up in Washington watching many of John Thompson Jr.'s Georgetown teams during the late 1980s and 1990s. A former newspaper and magazine reporter, Basen has also written several books about sports and sports issues. And Basen earned awards from the N. C. Press Association and Associated Press Sports Editors for work he did as a reporter with the *Charlotte Observer* newspaper in 2007 and 2008.